GODS AND GODDESSES

IN FOLK TALES FROM AROUND THE WORLD

RETOLD BY FIONA WATERS
ILLUSTRATED BY LIZ PYLE

Belitha Press

First published in the UK in 2001 by

Belitha Press Ltd
London House, Great Eastern Wharf,
Parkgate Road, London SW11 4NQ

ISBN 1 84138 317 1

British Library Cataloguing in Publication Data for
this book is available from the British Library.

Editors: Stephanie Turnbull, Russell McLean
Series editor: Mary-Jane Wilkins
Designer: Sarah Goodwin
Illustrator: Liz Pyle

Printed in China

10 9 8 7 6 5 4 3 2 1

CONTENTS

For Colin and Christina
with my love - F.W.

For George and
Ned with love - L.P.

THE SMALLEST GIFT IS THE MOST PRECIOUS

DEEP IN THE PROVINCE of Changteh in China, in an old walled town called Lin-Hsien, there is a crumbling and ancient monastery. In the innermost courtyard of the monastery there stands a huge statue of Buddha. It is made of bronze, but just over the heart there gleams a small copper coin. When the statue was cast the coin had virtually no value, but it became the most precious part of this particular Buddha.

A long time ago and more, there was a wealthy merchant in Lin-Hsien called Liu-Teh-Jong. He lived in a huge house with many rooms and gardens and, of course, he needed many servants to run this fine establishment. There were cooks and housekeepers and gardeners and cleaners and washerwomen and even a boy whose only job was to sweep the front doorstep whenever important guests arrived.

The least important of all was a little slave girl called Ya-teo. Her mother and father had sold her to Liu-Teh-Jong because they were too poor to keep her themselves. Ya-teo rose very early in the morning and from that moment on she never stopped until she dropped to sleep on her mat in the late evening, utterly worn out. She was at the beck and call of everyone and anyone,

and all day long she ran hither and thither, sweeping, cleaning and running errands. She was given food to eat by the cooks, and the gardener's wife made sure she had clothes to wear, but no-one really cared for her or even noticed that she was there most of the time.

One night Liu-Teh-Jong gave a great party for some of his merchant friends. Everyone had been frantically busy all day – the cooks especially became very hot and flustered and cross – but as dusk fell Ya-teo hid behind the great carved statue of a turtle that stood by the entrance to the house to watch the carriages arrive with the merchants and their wives. She gazed spellbound at the ladies in their wonderfully-coloured silks and jewellery, their tiny bound feet encased in embroidered slippers. They looked like fabulous butterflies and their laughter was like the tinkling of the wind chimes in the monastery cloisters.

In the morning, when Ya-teo was sweeping the inner courtyard after the party, she saw something glint on the ground. She bent down and found it was a cash, the smallest copper coin there was, virtually worthless to anyone else but a fortune to Ya-teo, who had never owned anything in her life. The person who had dropped it had probably not even bothered to look for it, so little was its value. Ya-teo rubbed it clean on her rough jacket and placed it carefully in her pocket.

All day long she felt the weight of the coin in her pocket and as she went about her tasks she thought of what she might buy with it. Perhaps the tiny little rice cakes that were sold in the market. Perhaps a wooden dragon from the toymaker, or some firecrackers from the firework factory. There were so many things she could think of. And when she went to bed she put the coin under her pillow and fell asleep still planning how she might spend it best.

But the next morning, a visitor arrived at the house and Ya-teo found her mind made up very easily.

Liu-Teh-Jong called everyone in his great household together, from his wives and his sons and daughters right through the cooks and housekeepers and gardeners and cleaners and washerwomen and even the boy whose only job was to sweep the front doorstep whenever important guests arrived, right down to little Ya-teo. A young monk from the monastery had come to talk to them about Buddha. Everyone loved Buddha, for he was a gentle teacher, wise beyond all knowledge and good above all others.

The monk told them that a huge statue of Buddha was to be erected in the monastery and everyone in Lin-Hsien was asked to contribute offerings towards the great cost. Everyone chattered excitedly and rushed to find gifts to give.

Liu-Teh-Jong gave several brimming chests of gold from his treasure vaults. The ladies of the house gave rings and bracelets and necklaces. Liu-Teh-Jong's mother gave her gold hair pins and combs. His sons gave huge heavy swords with jewelled hilts. His daughters gave their silver perfume bottles. The servants all gave precious and carefully hoarded coins. And Ya-teo realized happily that she too could make a contribution. She could give the copper cash. She fetched the coin from under her pillow and spoke to the monk.

'I found it while I was sweeping in the courtyard,' she said, 'and I was going to buy something for myself but now I wish to give it to the great Lord Buddha.' And she smiled happily as she held up the coin to the young monk. But to her dismay, the monk would not even pick it up from her outstretched hand.

'I couldn't spoil the image of the great Lord Buddha by putting such a small dirty coin in with all these riches!' and with a sweep of his hand he dashed the coin to the ground.

The monk strode back to the monastery without a backward glance or another word to Liu-Teh-Jong and his household.

Ya-teo picked up the small coin with tears in her eyes. For the first time in her life she had been able to offer a gift, and it had been rudely rejected. Ya-teo took her small copper coin and hid it under her pillow again. If it was not good enough for Buddha then perhaps she was not good enough to spend it either, so she gave up thinking about what she could buy and went back to her work with sadness in her heart.

Meanwhile at the monastery the great pile of treasure was growing. All the monks came back with more and more gold and silver and soon there was enough metal to make the statue. It was all melted down in a hot furnace and then poured slowly into the mould. After several days, when it had cooled, the casing was chipped away and the statue was revealed. All the monks gathered to watch and as the figure of Buddha emerged a great groan went up. For the statue looked terrible. The metal was dull and streaked and the surface looked rough.

'We must try again,' said the Father Abbot. 'Perhaps the furnace was not hot enough.' So they tried again, and they made the huge furnace so hot that it took even longer for the statue to cool in its mould. But this time was no better. The statue looked even worse. The Father Abbot went to pray quietly. After a while he returned and the monks gathered anxiously round him.

'I have to ask you if each gift that went to make up our statue was given with good grace and a humble heart?' he said quietly and looked at them all in turn. 'Only if this was done with love will our statue be worthy of the great Lord Buddha.'

Each and every monk spoke of the offerings they had received, and when it was the young monk's turn he told the Father Abbot about the generosity of Liu-Teh-Jong and his entire household. And then he remembered Ya-teo. He remembered her joy at being able to give something like everyone else. He remembered his scorn, and her eyes full of tears. And with his head hung low in shame, he told the Father Abbot how he had refused her gift.

'My son, this was not well done. She offered you all she had in the world and you scorned such a lowly gift,' said the Father Abbot. 'You must return in humility, and ask that she give you her little coin. Our statue needs Ya-teo's contribution.'

The proud young monk went back to Liu-Teh-Jong's house, and asked to speak to Ya-teo. On his knees he asked her forgiveness and begged her to give her treasure to the statue of Buddha. She ran to fetch the coin from under her pillow with a great singing joy in her heart.

The monk returned to the monastery and once more all the metal was melted down. This time Ya-teo's coin was placed at the heart of the furnace. When the mould was chipped away, the statue of Buddha was gleaming and perfect. And there, just over the great Lord's heart, was the little copper coin, no longer tarnished and dirty but gleaming proudly. From that time forth, people came from far and wide to see the statue and to hear the story of Ya-teo and her great gift.

Buddha decreed that people should live gentle lives, respecting each other no matter how poor or humble they might be, and dedicating their lives to good deeds and prayer.

How God Helped the Kikuyu

God made Africa with its great plains and high mountains and wide rivers. He covered the land with endless forests, filled with exotic flowers. He made all the animals, from the mighty lions to the swift antelopes. He made the beautiful egrets and the ugly vultures. And now he wanted someone to look after the land for him, so he summoned his three sons, Kamba, Masai and Kikuyu.

He told them that they were each to become the father of one tribe in the land he called Kenya. In his hands God held three things — a spear, a bow and a stick. Each son was to choose one of these objects to take with him when he descended to earth and his choice would decide what kind of life he was to lead.

Kamba chose first and he took the bow. He was sent to the forests where he became a hunter of animals, and was the father of the Chamba tribe. Masai came next and he chose the spear. God sent him to the great plains where he herded cattle, and he became the father of the Masai tribe.

Kikuyu was left with the stick. God explained that the stick was for digging holes in the earth to plant seeds to grow sweet potatoes and corn, so Kikuyu became a farmer. He found a land rich with fruit trees and deep grasslands growing on fertile soil. God had also provided a surprise for him. Under the fig trees, as if waiting for Kikuyu to arrive, was a beautiful girl. Her name was Moombi.

Moombi and Kikuyu were married and as the years passed they had nine children, all girls. Now Kikuyu loved his daughters beyond all else, but he wanted sons as well, so he returned to the volcano of Kere Nyaga to ask for God's advice, taking Moombi and their nine daughters with him.

'Father, I am well pleased with this land you have given me. It is rich and fertile and my crops are plentiful. The store huts are all full. I thank you for that. Moombi is an excellent wife to me, and I thank you for her also. We are greatly blessed above all with our beautiful daughters, all nine of them, and we thank you for them,' and he looked at God. 'But I also wish for sons to help me on the land.'

God smiled at his son. 'Of course you shall have sons. Listen carefully and do as I say, then you shall see what comes to pass. You must take a goat and a lamb and sacrifice them under a fig tree. You must pour their blood over the tree, and then Moombi and each of your daughters must make a burnt offering of the flesh of the animals under the tree. Then you must all return home. Go and do this with my blessing,' commanded God.

So Kikuyu did as he was told by God and then he and Moombi and the nine daughters made their way home. Imagine their astonishment when they were greeted by nine handsome and strong young men. Moombi quickly organized a great feast and there was much happiness that evening.

The next morning, Kikuyu took the nine young men down to the banks of the river, to fish as he told Moombi, but in reality he had thought of a plan in the night. He suggested that each of the young men might like to marry one of his daughters and, needless to say, the young men thought this a very fine idea. But Kikuyu had one important request. 'I love all my beautiful daughters and do not want to lose any of them. I must ask that when you are married you stay here with

me and Moombi. And when you have children they must bear the name of their mothers, not your names. The whole family must be called the family of Moombi,' demanded Kikuyu. The young men had no objections. Soon there was great rejoicing in the home of Kikuyu as nine weddings took place, all followed by several days of great celebration.

As the years rolled by the nine new families grew larger and in time both Kikuyu and Moombi died and their land was divided among the daughters and their families. But as even more time passed, the extended family grew so large that the land Kikuyu first called home could no longer support so many people. The nine daughters of Kikuyu and Moombi took their husbands and their children and each founded a separate tribe, every one of which bore the name of Moombi, as Kikuyu had originally asked.

In these tribes the women were the most important people. They were even more important than their husbands, and they punished their men severely for the smallest mistake. Before long the men began to object to this. They decided to answer back. But the daughters of Kikuyu and Moombi were very strong and determined, so the men had to think of a more devious plan to get their own way.

Then an unexpected piece of luck came their way. It became clear that every single daughter was expecting a baby and, of course, they were preoccupied with preparations for the birth of these children. The men made their move.

They took over as chiefs of the tribes and instead of being the Moombi, they insisted their people were now to be known as the Kikuyu. They decided that every man could have several wives and each separate family group was to be known by the man's name, not the wife's. Needless to say, the women were not prepared to put up with any of this and after a noisy meeting where they were so angry that they all tried to speak at once, they came up with a terrible plan to defeat their errant husbands.

The eldest daughter went to the men who were all sitting in the chief hut, very well pleased with how things had been turned around, and she uttered a dreadful threat.

'When our babies are born, we will only keep the girls. All the boy babies will be given away. And after that, we refuse to have any more babies at all!' and she turned on her heel and walked out.

Well, the men were stunned and horrified. They knew the women meant business and they also realized that with no more boy babies, the tribes would eventually die out. They realized that they had been outsmarted and the women had won. So they agreed to give up all their claims and once more the women were in charge. But they did agree that in honour of their much-loved father their people be known as the Kikuyu – as they are to this day.

Mount Kenya is a huge volcano, called Kere Nyaga by the Kikuyu. The Kikuyu believe that God chose Kere Nyaga, which means Mountain of Brightness or Mystery, as his home on earth.

ROMULUS
AND REMUS

NEARLY THREE THOUSAND YEARS AGO in the country now called Italy, there was a wise old King called Procas Silvius who ruled over the kingdom of Alba Longa. He had ruled well and wisely, but his life was drawing to a close and he wanted to ensure that peace would reign in Alba Longa after his death.

The problem was his two sons, who were as different as chalk from cheese. The elder son, who would rightfully inherit the throne, was called Numitor. He was a kind and thoughtful young man, well suited to rule after his father. But his younger brother, Amulius, was a jealous and ruthless boy who would stop at nothing to get what he wanted. The King decided to leave the throne to Numitor and all his wealth and lands to Amulius, in the hope that he would be content to leave Numitor to rule Alba Longa.

And so when Procas Silvius died, Numitor was declared King in succession to his father and Amulius found himself a very wealthy young man. But he wanted absolute power, so he seized the throne from Numitor, killed his two sons and banished Numitor and his wife and daughter from Alba Longa.

Now he had what he wanted and he ruled with a brutality that dismayed his advisers. But a nagging thought lurked at the back of his mind. What of Numitor's daughter, Rhea Silvia? He knew Numitor would never rise up against his own brother, but he could not be so sure that Rhea Silvia would be so accepting, especially if she married and had children of her own.

His first intention was to kill her, but then he thought of a far more cunning plan. He appointed her as a priestess of the goddess Vesta, a very great honour. Everyone could see that he had done well by his brother's daughter,

for as a Vestal Virgin she would be honoured and respected all her life. But more importantly for Amulius' intentions, she would be forbidden by law to marry and have children.

Rhea Silvia wept bitterly, for she did not want to be locked up all her life in a gloomy temple and she could see through her uncle's evil plans. But she had to accept her fate, so she became a Vestal Virgin. Finally Amulius felt safe.

But he was not aware that an even greater power was watching his ruthless treatment of his brother's family. The great god Mars looked down on Alba Longa from Mount Olympus and what he saw made him very angry. He decided it was time he stepped in. He warned Rhea Silvia in a dream that something very special was going to happen to her and told her she had his protection. She had this dream several nights running, and then she discovered she was going to have a baby.

Before long, she had to tell the High Priestess that she was pregnant. Rhea Silvia was dragged before Amulius to explain herself. Everyone was aghast. Rhea Silvia had broken the laws of the Vestal Virgins and, even worse, she claimed that the baby's father was Mars. She was locked up in a deep cellar and the servants were ordered to drown both her and the baby when it was born.

These were dark days for Rhea Silvia, but Mars sent her another dream telling her that all would be well. She was so gentle and kind, like her father Numitor, that the servants took pity on her and looked after her with great tenderness, resolving to save both her and her baby if they possibly could. When her time came, to her astonishment she gave birth to not one baby, but two, two beautiful strong and healthy boys. At dead of night, one of the bravest servants came to the cellar and took the babies away from the weeping Rhea Silvia. He laid them in a basket lined with rushes and soft sheep's wool and set it afloat on the mighty River Tiber.

The next morning the servant went to Amulius and told him that Rhea Silvia's baby had died. Amulius was so delighted that he did not ask any more questions but ordered Rhea Silvia to be kept imprisoned in the cellar. He thought then that all his problems were over and he soon forgot all about his brother Numitor and his family.

Meanwhile, Mars was keeping a close watch on his two sons. The basket floated gently down river, far away from the dangers of the palace. The babies slept on peacefully, unaware of their great journey.

As dawn broke the basket came to a rest in some rushes near the Palatine Hill. Before long the babies awoke and began to cry with hunger. One of the animals Mars loved especially was the wolf and so he had brought the basket to rest near a cave where a she-wolf had made a den for her cubs.

As she came down to the river for a drink, the wolf pricked her ears at the sound of the hungry babies. Her sharp nose soon found the basket. She leant in and, one by one, lifted the boys very gently in her teeth and carried them carefully back to the cave where she laid them beside her own cubs. She washed them all over with her warm tongue and fed them with her milk. Contented, the babies snuggled down in the warmth of the cubs and fell fast asleep. Thus they lived for many days and nights and grew into strong but wild little boys.

Mars realized that the children could not stay with the she-wolf for ever, so he made plans for them to come once more into the company of human beings. Near the she-wolf's cave there lived a shepherd, Faustulus, and his wife Laurentia. They had no children of their own, and lived very simply but contentedly. They grew their own vegetables and fruit, and looked after a flock of sheep for their master who was none other than the exiled Numitor.

Mars decided they would make excellent foster parents to his little sons. Faustulus knew the she-wolf had her den in the cave and he was always a little wary of her in case she tried to steal the sheep. He would watch her in the evenings when she let the cubs out to play in the setting sun. One evening he thought he heard human voices coming from the cave. He shook his head and decided his ears were playing tricks on him, but when the same thing happened the next night, he scrambled back to his hut where he told Laurentia all about it.

'You must be hearing things, husband,' she said, but she agreed to accompany him the following night to see if she could hear anything.

As they sat hidden behind some rocks, to their astonishment not only did they hear human voices, but two naked and very dirty little boys came tumbling out of the cave. They were laughing and playing with the wolf cubs. Faustulus and Laurentia crept away quietly and returned to their hut where they looked at each other in amazement.

'I am sure these children have been sent to us by the Gods,' said Faustulus. 'We must rescue them and bring them up as our own.'

So the next day, they waited until the she-wolf had gone hunting and then Faustulus crept into the cave and brought the children out. Carrying one each, Laurentia and Faustulus ran down the hill for dear life and, panting with their efforts, shut the door firmly behind them. The little boys were very dirty but were smiling and seemed happy and healthy enough. And so Faustulus and Laurentia acquired a ready-made family. They called the boys Romulus and Remus.

The boys soon adapted to their new way of life and as the years passed they grew into strong, handsome young men. They helped Faustulus and Laurentia with the sheep and hunted rabbits and birds for food in the woods. They never quite lost their wild ways though and, wanting adventure, would attack the local bandits and take the valuables they had stolen from others. But one day the bandits surprised them in an ambush and they were dragged before Numitor.

'We demand that you punish these youths,' said the chief of the bandits, who had smartened himself up in the hope that Numitor would give him a reward for bringing the two troublemakers to justice. He made no mention of his own role in the stealing.

But Numitor just stared intently at Romulus and Remus, unable to believe his eyes. The resemblance to his lost daughter Rhea Silvia was so overwhelming that at first he was lost for words. Then he shook himself and dismissed the bandits, who stumped off crossly without their expected reward, and asked to see the father of the two young men who stood in front of him.

'Tell me about your sons,' he asked Faustulus gently. 'They remind me strangely of someone I loved very much long ago.'

'Sir, my wife Laurentia and I have brought up Romulus and Remus as our own, but they are not of our flesh and blood,' said Faustulus, and he told the incredible story of how he had found the boys in the she-wolf's den. With tears in his eyes, Numitor embraced his grandsons, then sat down to tell them who they were and what had happened to their family.

'Amulius has cheated us of our birthright,' cried Romulus.

'We must right this terrible wrong,' shouted Remus, and the two brothers strode off to rally their friends to help. A few nights later, they stormed the palace and killed the wicked Amulius, to the great delight of most of the courtiers and servants. Amulius had not been much loved.

Rhea Silvia was released from her prison in the cellar and reunited with her beloved sons. Numitor was restored to the throne, and he ruled for many years. Alba Longa was a happy country once more. And Mars looked down from Mount Olympus with a smile playing on his lips. Justice had been done.

Romulus and Remus were content for a while, but then they grew restless. Numitor suggested they build a new city on the spot where they were found by the she-wolf. With their usual energy they threw themselves into this new project, and in time the city was built at the foot of the Palatine Hill, on the banks of the mighty Tiber.

There were wide streets and great baths, and a huge temple to Mars, the God of War who had watched over them so carefully. But the brothers could not agree what to call their fine city, and they quarrelled bitterly. Perhaps it was the she-wolf's milk that made them a little wild still, but they came to blows and in a rage Romulus killed his brother Remus. Thus it was that the new city acquired the name it still goes by – Rome.

Rome is reputed to have been built in 753 BC. It grew until it was the capital of Italy and is still one of the greatest cities in the world.

THE FINGER MEN

LONG, LONG AGO, when the moon was young and the earth new, the Four Gods of the Maya were resting, exhausted by the labour of creating the earth. They had filled deep oceans and raised mighty mountains. They had planted hot jungles and spread dry sandy plains. They had filled the seas with fish, and the forests with birds and butterflies, and the plains with animals. They had blown up mighty winds and tumbling clouds, and had thrown rain into the skies. They had placed the hot sun in the blue sky of day, and the cold moon into the darkness of night.

As they lay looking down on earth, they were well pleased with their efforts, but they realized one thing was missing. There were no people on this new earth. No people to praise and worship the gods for all their efforts.

They talked long into the night, trying to decide what they should use to create people. They had used all the fur on the animals, all the feathers for the birds and all the scales for the fish. They decided to try mud.

They mixed sand from the plains with water from the oceans and shaped it roughly into the form of a little man. With a stick they drew eyes and a mouth and a nose, and they left the little man in the sun to dry. He looked very fine, and the Four Gods were pleased with their new man. But then it rained and, of course, the little figure crumbled away.

They thought again. This time they decided man should be made from wood. Taking a dry branch, they carefully carved the figure, giving him legs and arms, fingers and toes, a small nose and mouth and hollowed-out eyes and ears. The figure was much more delicate than the mud man. They placed him on the water at the ocean edge and he floated, and didn't crumble away.

The Four Gods were pleased. That evening as they lay warming themselves by a big blazing fire, the gods placed the wooden man close to the burning embers. But a log tumbled out of the fire and fell on to the wooden man, and he was quickly burnt until nothing remained but a pile of ash.

The gods were perplexed. What else could they use? Walking by the river next day, a glinting stone under the water caught the eye of the Third God. He plunged in his arm and brought out a gleaming nugget of gold. They all agreed that here, finally, was the ideal material to create their man.

The figure when it was finished looked splendid. He had tumbling golden hair, flashing golden eyes and strong golden arms and legs. When the gods put him in water, he did not dissolve. When they placed him at the heart of their fire, he did not burn, indeed he came out burnished and looking even more splendid.

Now they had the ideal man, and they lost no time in telling him how hard they had worked and how splendid their earth was. But the golden man did not reply. They showed him the deep oceans and the mighty mountains. They showed him the jungles and the plains. But still the golden man looked neither to right nor left, and spoke not a word.

They held him up to hear the song of the birds and to see the brightly-coloured butterflies. They showed him the splendours of all the wild animals. But never a word of praise did the golden man utter. The Four Gods were annoyed. All the beauty and magnificence of their creation of earth was unnoticed and no words of gratitude were to be heard. The golden man was clearly not going to praise them as they had hoped and so they threw him aside in anger.

Now the Fourth God was more thoughtful than the others. He saw that if they were to create people, they had to use something living, not inanimate objects like wood or gold. So he grasped a sharp knife, and quickly chopped off all the fingers of his left hand.

The fingers ran off as fast as ever they could and hid under the lush leaves of the jungle. The Four Gods could not move fast enough to catch them, and so they didn't try the fingers in the water or the fire. The fingers found food to eat and shelter in the forest, and thus they became the first people.

Soon there were thousands of them but still the Four Gods did not have anyone to praise their work, for the finger people could not talk. The Four Gods gave up and, exhausted with their efforts and not a little grumpy at their failure to find praise, they fell into a deep, deep sleep.

The finger people were endlessly busy. They ran hither and thither, collecting water to drink and finding out what they could cook and eat. They built rough shelters under the trees in the jungle and soon learned which animals were friendly, and which were not.

One day, they found the golden man, lying in the undergrowth where the gods had thrown him in their irritation. His gold was dull and he was covered in weeds and insects. The finger people were very puzzled, and not a little frightened by this strange creature that did not blink or smile. They offered him water to drink and food to eat but he left it untouched. He never moved. They crept up cautiously until they were able to touch him, but oh how cold he was! He made the finger people tremble with the chill that came off his unmoving body. And they all ran away, back to their shelters in the jungle.

But the bolder ones realized that the golden man might be important, so they crept back the next day. He was still lying there in exactly the same position as before. The food and water lay untouched, and there was no sign of recognition in his cold golden eyes.

The finger people dragged the golden man into the open where they crowded round him excitedly. They could see he was very beautiful and they wondered why he had been lying in the undergrowth. They decided he must be important somehow, and they began to stroke and polish his hard surface. And, of course, he began to shine and gleam, so they polished him even more.

Gradually the surface of the golden man grew warm, and as it grew warmer he began to look more alive.

Every day, the finger people came to polish the golden man until he glittered like the sun herself. She sent her golden rays down to the man lying on the grass, and as the heat touched the golden man he began to speak, to the astonishment of the finger people. The words of praise and gratitude that the Four Gods had whispered in his hard golden ear poured from his mouth.

His words rang round the mountains and across the oceans, and reached the ears of the Four Gods, who were still fast asleep and snoring. They awoke suddenly. They sat up and rubbed their eyes. Before them stood thousands of the finger people, and the gods saw how they had multiplied and looked after themselves, and they were very pleased.

They heard the words of praise and gratitude pouring out from the golden man, and they were even more pleased. And they decided that people would be created the same as the finger people and the golden man for ever more. The finger people would help the golden people survive, and the golden people would protect the finger people.

The golden people would always be rich, the finger people would always be poor. But the first law the Four Gods made was that no rich man might enter heaven unless he was hand in hand with a poor man. Finally the Four Gods were able to glory in their land, with words of praise echoing in their ears for ever more. The sacrifice of the Fourth God had been worthwhile.

The Mayans arrived in Central America around 2500 BC and went on to found the greatest of the ancient civilizations of the continent. Many of their myths and legends were written down after the Spanish Conquest.

VISHNU APPEARS AS A FISH

MANU, THE SON OF SURYA, the God of the Sun, was washing himself in the river early one morning. As he scooped up the water to splash his face, he felt something move in his hands. When he looked down, he saw that it was a tiny fish. As he bent down to return the fish to the river, to his astonishment it spoke to him.

'Please do not put me back in the river, Manu,' said the fish in a clear voice that was like water splashing. 'I am so very small that I will be eaten up by another bigger fish if you do not save me.'

Manu was sure the fish must be magical and so he thought he should be very careful what he did next. He could see the river was teeming with fish and most of them were indeed very much bigger than the little creature cupped in his hands. So he dropped the tiny fish into the earthenware pot he had brought intending to fill it with water to take back to the house. He placed the pot in the shade of the verandah and went about his daily tasks.

When he came home that night, he was staggered to see the fish had grown so big that already the pot was far too small for it. He found a glass tank and, putting the fish inside, went to bed after saying his prayers.

In the morning he found the fish had grown so much during the night that the water was overflowing, and the fish's head and tail were flapping outside the tank. Carefully he carried the fish down to the lake in his garden and it swam around most cheerfully.

But that night when Manu returned home, the fish had become an absolute monster and was too large even for the lake.

'You must take me to the ocean, Manu,' said the fish. 'Now that I am no longer so tiny I shall survive quite well.'

So Manu took the fish down to the vast ocean and released it. As he let go of it, the fish reared up on its tail and spoke once more to Manu.

'My name is Matsya, and because you have saved my life I shall save yours. One year from now to the very day, a great flood will come and all the land will be covered. Everyone will drown, all the people and all the creatures and birds. To save yourself you must build a big boat, and when the time of the flood draws near you must get into the boat and with you take seven wise men. You must also take two of every kind of animal and bird and insect. Lastly, make sure you have collected a seed of every plant and tree,' and with that the fish dived deep to the bottom of the ocean.

Manu wasted no time in doing what Matsya had told him. He drew up plans for a huge boat, with compartments for all the animals and the seven wise men, and special drawers for all the seeds. He asked several of his friends to help him build the boat but they just laughed at him. They thought he was mad. But Manu went about building the boat with great determination, chopping down trees, sawing them into planks and stacking the wood in great heaps. Every night in his prayers, he remembered Matsya and thanked him for his warning.

It took very nearly the year to construct the boat and Manu had to work late into the night to ensure it was ready in time. Dark clouds were rolling across the sky and thunder rumbled in the distance as he hammered in the last of the nails. He then rounded up two each

of all the animals and birds and insects he could find, and led them on to the boat. They settled into their compartments contentedly, for animals are very wise, and they knew that something terrible was about to happen.

Manu found seven wise men and persuaded them to climb on board the boat, while all around people mocked and jeered, ignoring the huge raindrops that had begun to fall. And then, exactly a year to the day since Manu had released Matsya into the ocean, the sky grew black, lightning struck and rain fell in a deluge. Manu just managed to run on board in time as the boat began to float on the flood water.

For days on end the boat floated along on the rising waters. Eventually nothing could be seen above the water. Houses, trees and even hills disappeared. The last thing to go under was the highest mountain. As far as the eye could see there was nothing but water and then more water. Manu had no idea which direction they were travelling in, and at first he was content to drift along, but as the days stretched into weeks and the weeks into months he began to be anxious.

Manu took to standing on the deck of the boat, constantly looking towards the horizon to see if there was any sign of land. Then one day he felt a great bump against the side of the boat. He rushed to look over and there he saw a gigantic fish. It was Matsya. He was now covered in golden scales and had a huge horn in the centre of his head.

'Well done, Manu!' he said. 'I see you have done as I told you. Now you must obey me once more. Loop a rope round my horn and I will tow the boat through the flood,' and Manu did as he was bid. Matsya swam strongly forward and the boat followed silently through the waters. Matsya towed the boat for years and years, during which time Manu never gave up watching the horizon and never gave up saying a special prayer for Matsya every night.

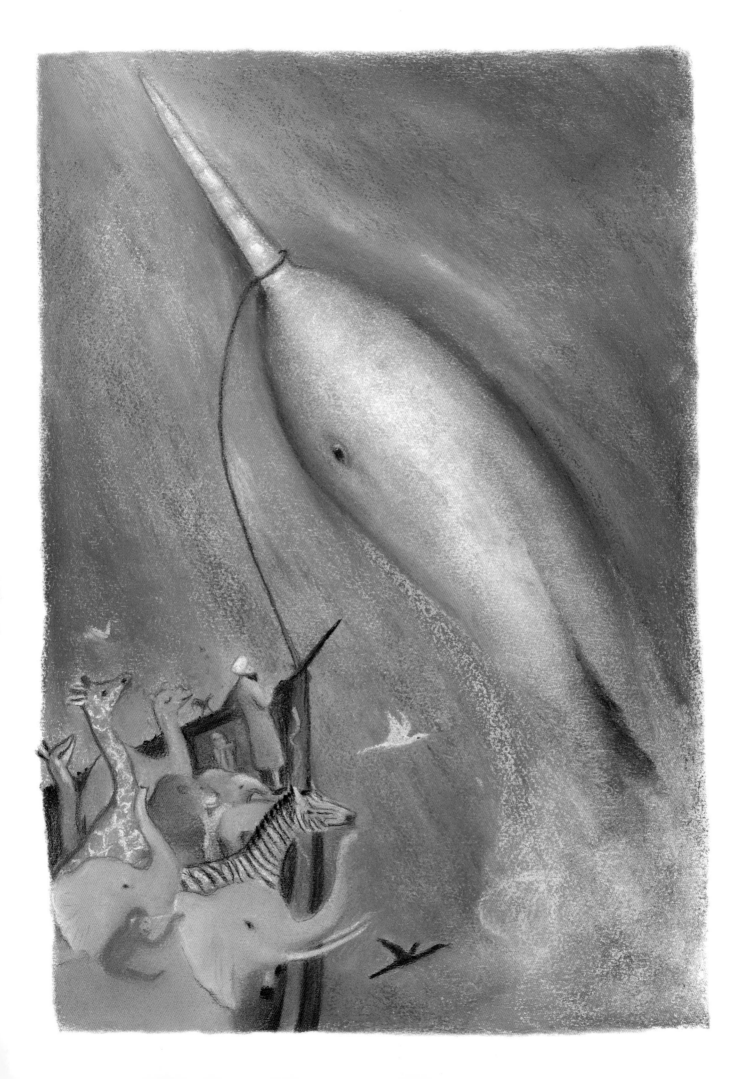

One day, at long, long last Manu gave a great cry of joy. There in the far distance he could just make out the jagged peak of a mountain. Matsya towed the boat closer as all the animals and the birds and the insects, and the seven wise men, crowded round Manu on the deck. The rocks were the tips of the mighty Himalayas, the highest mountains in the world. Matsya swam up close and told Manu to loop the rope round a rock.

'When the waters start to go down, which they will do very soon, the boat will float gently down too. Then you and the seven wise men and all the animals and all the birds and all the insects will be able to walk on the land again,' said Matsya.

And so it happened. First the mountains, then the high meadows, then the first trees and finally the fields were uncovered. Manu let the animals out in their pairs and they kicked up their heels and raced round and round, delighted to be free once more. Then he released the birds high into the sky and they swooped and wheeled and sang in their great delight. Finally he let the insects out, once the animals had settled down and their great feet no longer threatened to crush the tiny ants. He left the boat himself with the wise men and they began the task of replanting the earth with all the seeds Manu had stored so carefully.

But first they built a temple to Matsya, who had saved them from the destruction of the earth and guided them through the waters for all those years. And when it was finished they all gathered for a great festival of dedication. Manu was just about to speak when there came a mighty rushing wind and a great shaft of light from the heavens. Suddenly the great God Vishnu himself was in their midst, blessing the animals and the birds and the insects. And he blessed the wise men and their seeds, and finally he came to Manu.

'You will be the first of the new race for only you survive. I will send you a beautiful girl to be your wife and you will have many children and even more grandchildren. Your families will have my protection forever,' and so saying Vishnu vanished. He was utterly weary after all his hard work as the fish Matsya. He called on the Goddesses Lakshmi and Sarasvati to prepare his couch and he sank into a deep sleep from which he did not wake for thousands of years.

And as for Manu, he and his wife did have many children and their descendants are the ancestors of all Hindus.

Vishnu is the most important of the Hindu gods. He had to come to earth in ten separate incarnations to save the world and this is the story of his first visit. He always came in disguise, as it would be bad luck for people to see him in all his glory.

SUSANO AND THE SUN GODDESS

LONG, LONG AGO IZANAGI, the God of the Air, met Izanami, the Goddess of the Clouds, on a floating bridge in heaven. She was as fair as the high summer clouds and he was as brave as the winter wind, and they fell in love. They decided to marry. But first they had to create earth so they might leave the floating bridge and live below the clouds and the winds.

Out of the dark chaos below they made a kingdom of eight islands which they called Japan and there they produced many children. The most beautiful of all was Amaterasu, the Sun Goddess, whose light lit the whole world. But the one who troubled them most was Susano, the Storm God.

Susano was a difficult child, always gloomy and sneaking around in the darkness. When he was cross, he would stamp about furiously, making everyone's life a misery. His fierce tears of anger would fall to earth and where they fell the grass would wither and flowers would fade and die.

When he was feeling particularly spiteful he would send down great rain storms that would wash away the tender rice shoots on the terraces. Sometimes he blew up huge winds that tore all the fruit from the trees in the orchards. Time and time again Izanagi would punish him for his bad behaviour. Time and time again Amaterasu would forgive him for all the damage he caused.

But Susano would not change his behaviour, in fact he grew more and more unpleasant until one day even gentle,

32

forgiving Amaterasu had had
enough. In a huge rage, Susano
flung his horse through the
roof of the sacred temple
where Amaterasu sat with
her hand maidens. The
horse broke its neck in
the fall and Amaterasu
and her maidens fled
in distress and terror.

They hid in a
deep and dark cave.
They stopped up
the entrance so no
one could possibly
come in. Of course,
no light could come
out of the cave
either, and the entire
earth was covered in utter
darkness and the world grew miserable.

The crops shrivelled in the fields and nothing would grow. The animals
of the fields and the birds in the sky all lay down and refused to move until the
sun shone again. In a towering rage, Izanagi banished the unruly Storm God
to the underworld and told him he never wished to see his face again. Susano
just laughed.

Long dark months passed, and still Amaterasu and her maidens would not
leave the safety of their dreary cave. The rice fields lay muddy and not a green
shoot was to be seen. The pears grew rotten on the branches of the trees and the
ground was littered with the skeletons of dead animals.

The great gods and goddesses of the heavens (and there were eight hundred of them all told) gathered for a meeting to decide what to do. They talked and argued all through one day and one night and all through another day before they managed to devise a plan to coax Amaterasu out of her cave.

It was Omorikane, probably the wisest god of all, who finally came up with a solution. He sent messengers to all four corners of the earth to bring back as many precious jewels as they could find. As swift as the winds they flew, and came back with great caskets, brimful with rubies and emeralds and sapphires and opals and diamonds. And Omorikane asked ten of the gods to thread the jewels into a great, long, glittering necklace.

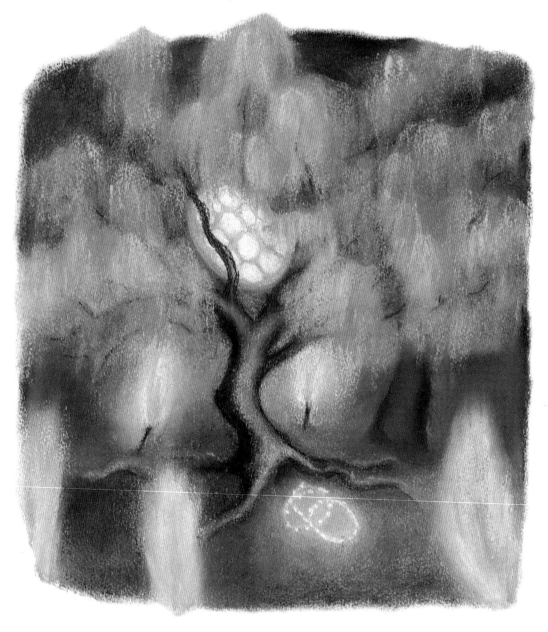

Then he sent his messengers to the deepest seas and asked them to bring back the shiniest mother-of-pearl shells they could find. And Omorikane asked ten more of the gods to set the shells into a great circle of wood and to polish them till they gave out a reflection like a huge mirror.

Then he sent his messengers to the sacred grove and begged a magical tree from the Goddess of the Woods which they planted right in front of the cave where Amaterasu and her maidens were hiding. The shell mirror was hidden in its branches, and the long glittering necklace of precious jewels was coiled at the foot of its slender trunk. The God of Fire provided tall flaring torches which were placed in a wide circle round the tree.

Then the Goddess of Dawn, whose beauty was only matched by Amaterasu herself, began dancing under the branches of the sacred tree outside the cave. All the other gods and goddesses gathered round the entrance to the cave, and as the Goddess of Dawn weaved and spun in her intricate dance, they applauded her grace and gasped at the speed of her tiny feet.

Now eight hundred gods and goddesses can make quite a bit of noise and before long, a tiny crack appeared in the entrance to the cave and a face peered cautiously out. It was one of Amaterasu's hand maidens.

She saw all the gods and goddesses, and she saw the Goddess of Dawn dancing and then she disappeared back into the cave. The gods and goddesses all sighed at once, and the sound was like a summer wind through the leafy trees. Omorikane smiled, and asked the Goddess of Dawn to continue her dance.

Faster and faster her feet twirled. The gods and goddesses clapped softly, and the sound was like the beating of the wings of a thousand swallows, and soon a new face was to be seen in the entrance to the cave. It was another of Amaterasu's hand maidens. She came further out of the cave, and stood looking at the whirling Goddess of Dawn. She saw all the happy faces of the gods and goddesses, she heard their clapping hands and then she too disappeared back into the cave. Omorikane smiled even more as he asked the Goddess of Dawn to dance just a little longer.

Once again she danced with the speed of light as the watching gods and goddesses clapped loudly and stamped their feet in appreciation. This time the entrance to the cave was opened wide and there stood Amaterasu herself. The Goddess of Dawn stopped dancing, and everyone held their breath.

Amaterasu had caught sight of the shell mirror glinting in the branches of the sacred tree. She stepped forward, fascinated by its gleaming surface. It had been so very dark in the cave, and she suddenly realized that she was looking at herself. And as the mirror caught her reflection it began to glow. Amaterasu took a few more steps forward and as she did so, two of the gods uncoiled the great necklace of precious jewels and stretched it right across the entrance to the cave to stop Amaterasu from going back in.

The glow from the mirror increased in radiance and with a shout of joy the gods and goddesses realized that their Sun Goddess was shining again. The warmth of her smile grew and grew, and the earth was restored. It did not take long for the land to recover. As the sun shone so the crops flourished, the trees bore fruit, the animals bounded across the fields and the birds flew in the sky.

Izanagi and Izanami rejoiced to see their beautiful daughter restored to them in all her radiance, and they were content that their kingdom of eight islands was once more a happy and fertile place. As for Susano, he stormed and raged in the underworld and such was his power that for ever after he could still cause huge tempests and floods, but he never teased his sister again.

The ancient religion of Japan is Shinto, and great importance is given to the kami, or spirits, who live in the fields and rivers. The greatest kami of all is the Goddess of the Sun, Amaterasu, who is also believed to be the ancestor of all the Japanese emperors.

Midir the Proud and Fair Etain

The God Midir, ruler of Bri Leith, had a wife called Fuamnach, but when he first saw the mortal girl Etain he fell hopelessly in love with her. She was so beautiful that she was known throughout the land for her fair skin and her blue eyes, blue as the wild bluebells that grew in the forest.

Midir married Etain after a whirlwind courtship and carried her home to where a less-than-pleased Fuamnach took an instant dislike to her.

For a short time, Fuamnach tried to hide her bitter jealousy, but Midir was so besotted with Etain that he would hardly leave her side. Fuamnach had powerful magic of her own, and one day she decided to get rid of her young and beautiful rival.

Etain was walking alone by the side of the river, watching the fish swim in the clear water, when Fuamnach crept up behind her and with a powerful spell turned her into a dragonfly. As the dragonfly skimmed low over the water, her wings iridescent in the sunlight, Fuamnach laughed in triumph and returned home. Midir was broken-hearted when he found out what had happened, but he was powerless to undo Fuamnach's spell as she had used very old and powerful magic.

One day a glittering dragonfly appeared, swooping and fluttering by Midir's head. He realized it must be Etain, and he was overjoyed, but black was the heart of Fuamnach by this time. She was furious that she had not managed to get rid of Etain completely, so she called on her magic again.

A huge gust of wind rushed through Bri Leith and the dragonfly was blown up, up into the sky. The wind blew on and on, over the hills and down to the sea where it subsided as quickly as it had blown up. The battered and bruised dragonfly fell to the shore where the waves crashed and the sand drifted, and there she lay soaked and covered in salt.

Seven long years passed. Fuamnach thought she need fear her rival no more. Midir never passed a day without thinking of Etain but he had no idea what had happened to her. And so they lived together, Fuamnach realizing that she had still lost Midir.

Now in a gorgeous palace a little to the north of Dublin lived Angus of the Birds, the God of Love. One day he was walking along the shore and his eye was caught by a shimmer among the rocks. It was the

dragonfly. Angus could see that this was no ordinary dragonfly, for the people of the faery can never hide from each other, so he picked her up and took her home. He too could not undo the magic of Fuamnach, but he was able to release Etain from the spell at dusk and so until dawn she was able to regain her human form. But as soon as the sun rose, she changed back into a dragonfly. Angus made her a crystal cage, covered with sweet-smelling honeysuckle, where she could shelter during the day.

It did not take long for the news of the fabulous dragonfly who turned into a beautiful maiden by night to reach Bri Leith and the ears of both Midir and Fuamnach. Midir set off immediately to reclaim his lost love, but Fuamnach again thwarted him. She stole the cage and tossed the dragonfly once more high into the skies.

This time the mighty wind blew her all the way to Ulster and down the chimney into the feasting hall of a chieftain. She fluttered into a goblet of wine that the mistress of the house, Etar, was drinking from and was swallowed before Etar even noticed. But that was not the end of Etain.

Nine months later, Etar gave birth to a tiny baby daughter. She had fair skin and blue eyes, blue as the wild bluebells that grew in the forest, and Etar called her Etain, a choice that surprised her husband the chieftain because it was not a family name. But Etar said she had had a strange dream in which Angus the God of Love had appeared to her and told her this was to be the name of her baby.

Now although she had the same name as before, Etain had no memory of her former life as a dragonfly. She grew into the most beautiful young woman whose laughter filled the house all day long.

The High King of Ireland at that time was Eochaid Airem and his advisers told him he must marry if he was to maintain his powerful position as head of all Ireland. There was no one at court that Eochaid Airem wished to marry, so he sent his bravest warriors the length and breadth of the land to find a suitable maiden.

Before long they brought back reports of the beauty of Etain, and as soon as he saw her, Eochaid knew he need look no further and they were married within a few days. Once again the news travelled quickly and in Bri Leith Midir realized that the king's new bride was none other than his beloved Etain.

With no thought as to how he was to achieve his heart's desire to have her by his side once more, Midir set off to court to speak to Etain. He told her that she was first and foremost his wife and asked her to return to Bri Leith with him. She still remembered nothing of her previous life and told Midir that if he really loved her he would never have let her go. In vain he tried to explain about Fuamnach's magic, but this only made her even more angry. As far as she was concerned, Midir was at fault for having upset Fuamnach in the first place and she had no intention of leaving her new husband, who was after all the High King of Ireland. Midir left the court in despair.

But he returned a few days later and sought out the High King. Eochaid had a reputation as a great chess player and Midir challenged him to a game. The king asked what the stakes were to be, and Midir suggested that the loser should pay whatever the winner asked for, no matter how difficult or strange the request should be. And so the match began.

Now what the High King did not know was that his opponent had never been beaten in a game before. But Midir had a cunning ploy. He let the king win the game, and he enjoyed it so much that Eochaid challenged Midir to another game.

Again, Midir let the king win, and again Eochaid challenged for a third game. This time, Midir did not let the king win and Eochaid was forced to concede the game. Midir asked for a simple thing – a kiss from the king's new bride. All unsuspecting, a blushing Etain was led in to the great hall. She frowned when she saw who was to claim this kiss, but at the touch of Midir's lips upon hers, all her memory came flooding back.

Before any of the king's guards could reach for their swords, Midir swung Etain up into his arms and ran out of the great hall, down the steps of the courtyard and over the drawbridge out into the forest. The king and his warriors ran after them but there was no sign of either Midir or Etain. They seemed to have vanished into thin air. As they gazed around in astonishment, they heard the beat of great wings.

There, high over the palace, were two pure white swans, flying wing tip to wing tip, linked by a golden chain round their necks. Thus Midir won back Etain and they lived for ever more in great peace at Bri Leith. No one knows what happened to Fuamnach.

In the Celtic tradition, gods and goddesses could take on the form of animals and birds, and also absorb the characteristics of the creatures. Swans were thought to be birds of healing and purity, bringing love and joy to all.

SADKO AND THE TSAR OF THE SEA

LONG AGO, WHEN WOLVES still roamed the vast steppes of Russia, a great city flourished on the shores of Lake Ilmen near the Baltic coast. It was called Novgorod. The harbour was busy with ships from Venice and Peking, India and Norway, and the market was always a hubbub of strange sights and sounds and smells. Wealthy merchants bought and sold cargoes of gold and silver, costly jewels, rich fabrics and furs, spices and rare perfumes.

Sadko the minstrel was not rich and he didn't live in a grand house, and he certainly didn't have a fleet of sailing ships carrying rich cargoes. But he did own a very old gusle, a musical instrument rather like a harp. It had belonged to his great-grandfather, and Sadko had been taught to play by his father.

Sadko's gusle was very beautiful. It was made of the finest maple wood which had become a deep rich colour over the years. A peg held the string taut at the neck of the gusle, and at the top was an ornately-carved figure of a horseman, the horse's head worn smooth by years of handling. Sadko played at the feasts the merchants gave whenever their ships came home well-laden. By the end of an evening his hat was always brimming with coins and he did not go hungry that night.

But there came a time when the merchants grew gloomy. Storms kept their ships from port or, worse still, some were lost at sea for ever. Sadko was not asked to play any more for there were no feasts, and as his small bag of money dwindled he grew hungrier. The day came when he took the last coin from his bag and bought a loaf of rough black bread. As night fell, he sat on the shores of Lake Ilmen, chewing the dry bread and gazing out across the moonlit water. He reached for his gusle and began playing a sad little tune.

As the clear notes rang out across the water, a voice joined in. Sadko was frightened at first for he thought it must be a rusalka, one of the water sprites who were said to be the lost souls of drowned maidens. But he played on bravely, and as he played, a girl gradually rose from the dark water. Her hair fell in a shimmering curtain to her knees, and her eyes were the deepest sea-blue Sadko had ever seen. She wore a dress of glistening seaweed and round her neck hung a necklace of tiny pink seashells. Round her head she wore a crown of sea-washed gold coins. She was Volkhova, the daughter of the Tsar of the Sea.

'Please don't stop playing, Sadko,' she said, and her voice was like the whisper of gentle waves upon the shore. 'You play so well.'

Sadko played again. Sad songs, happy songs, noble songs – he played and played all night, and he never took his eyes off Volkhova. Then, as the first fingers of dawn crept over the horizon, she put a finger to her lips and Sadko stopped.

'I must return to my father, the Tsar of the Sea,' she whispered, 'but you will be rewarded for your beautiful music.' She took three golden coins from her crown and threw them deep into the lake. 'Cast a net here tonight, and you will find three fish with golden fins. They will bring you great wealth, but you must remember they are a gift from my father, the Tsar of the Sea. Farewell, Sadko. I will remember your music always.' And with the smallest ripple she was gone.

Sadko shook his head. Had he been dreaming? But at his feet lay a small pink shell and he knew it had all been real. He hurried back into the city and sought out his friend, Mikula the fisherman.

'I must borrow your net tonight!' Sadko cried and explained what had happened. Mikula, of course, did not believe a word of Sadko's improbable tale. Nevertheless he promised to lend Sadko his nets that evening, after his day's fishing was over. In the meantime, Mikula told everyone about Sadko's crazy notion. By the time evening came round, quite a crowd had gathered, all of them ready to laugh at Sadko and his silly story.

Sadko said nothing as he cast the net far out into the lake. The water was silver in the moonlight as it had been the night before. The net lay on the surface of the water, rippling gently as the water moved. The people began to be restless and impatient. Still Sadko said nothing. Still the net lay in the moonlight. People began to drift back to the city as clearly nothing out of the ordinary was going to happen. Still Sadko said nothing. His head was full of the beauty of Volkhova.

Suddenly, the water of the lake began to churn and boil. The few people left on the shore started to their feet, and a slow smile crept over Sadko's face. He pulled the net in slowly and there lay three glistening fish. Their fins were of the purest gold.

Sadko was a wise young man and he put his wealth to good use. Before long, he had a fleet of sailing ships travelling the world, looking for rare and splendid treasures. He became rich beyond his wildest dreams, but he never forgot the beautiful Volkhova. Nor did he forget to whom he owed his wealth. Whenever he crossed the oceans, he always raised a glass to toast the Tsar of the Sea to ensure fair winds and a calm sea. Nor did he forget Mikula. He gave him a whole fleet of fishing boats and more nets than he could count. And so many years passed.

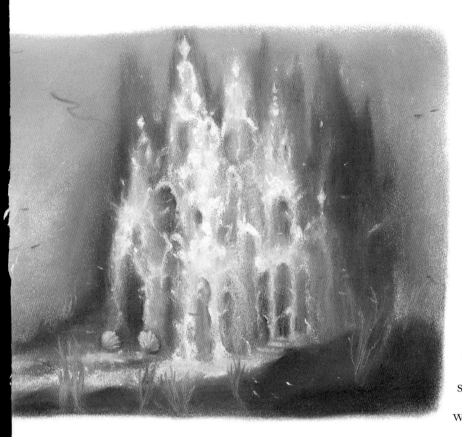

One autumn, Sadko was sailing home on his favourite ship. It had been a successful voyage, and the ship was laden with gold and silver in great chests, baskets of sea pearls from the China Seas, cinnamon and nutmeg from the spice route, and fine woven shawls from India. All was well until the ship suddenly stopped. The sails were full of wind and the waves splashed against the sides of the boat, but the ship remained motionless. The sailors had never experienced anything like this before and they knew some supernatural force was to blame.

With a sinking heart, Sadko remembered that he had not toasted the health of the Tsar of the Sea, as he had been too busy counting the chests of gold and silver. He did not want his sailors to die with him so he told them they must sail on without him. He called for pen and parchment and wrote his will, leaving all his wealth divided among his sailors and their families, and his faithful friend Mikula. Then, grasping only his beloved gusle in his hand, he leapt over the side of the ship and plunged deep into the sea.

Down, down he sank into the blue water. He had no sensation of drowning and as he looked around at all the strange and wonderful sea creatures, he felt quite unafraid. Deeper and deeper, down he went until he landed on the ocean bed with a bump. There in front of him was the most gorgeous palace. It was made of coral and richly decorated with shells and glittering pebbles. Fountains played in the courtyards, and brilliantly-coloured fish darted through the archways. The floors were covered in gleaming pearls and great gardens of gently waving fronds of seaweed surrounded the walls. Seahorses formed a guard round a great scallop shell throne, and there sat the Tsar of the Sea, frowning terribly. At his feet sat Volkhova.

'Well, Sadko, we meet at last,' said the Tsar and his voice rumbled like the sound of a great shingle beach being sucked back by the tide. 'My daughter has pleaded with me to save your life. She tells me you are a great musician, so now you must play for me,' he commanded.

So Sadko took up his gusle and began to play. The Tsar of the Sea began to smile, and his feet began to tap in time to the tune. As the music grew wilder, he leapt to his feet and began whirling round and round. He danced and danced, and great waves churned round and round in the sea. Far above, on the surface of the water, it was as if a great storm had arisen. Waves crashed and winds howled, and ships were tossed about as if they were toys. Still Sadko played for dear life and the Tsar of the Sea danced and whirled without pause. Goodness knows what damage might have been caused had Sadko not suddenly heard a voice in his ear. It was Saint Nikolai, the patron saint of sailors.

'Sadko! Sadko! Stop playing or we will all be drowned,' he shouted.

'I cannot stop,' cried Sadko. 'The Tsar is angry with me and has commanded that I play for him.'

'You must break your gusle, then he cannot make you play on,' said Saint Nikolai.

Sadko did not hesitate. He lifted his precious gusle high above his head, and smashed it into smithereens.

There was a sudden great silence. The waves stilled. The Tsar stopped whirling round. Volkhova looked at Sadko with her eyes full of tears. She knew that he valued his gusle above all his great riches. Saint Nikolai bowed towards the Tsar and took Sadko by the hand.

'Sadko has paid dearly for his one lapse, mighty Tsar. I ask you to release him,' he said sternly.

The Tsar smiled at them both.

'I have never heard such music in all my life. Thank you, Sadko. You have indeed redeemed yourself. I release you back to your life above the waves.'

But as he finished speaking, Volkhova flung herself at her father's feet.

'Dear Father, please may I go with Sadko? I have longed for his company again ever since we first met by the shores of Lake Ilmen.'

Sadko was astonished by her words, and his heart leapt for joy. But how would she live on dry land, and how could he bear never to play music to her ever again?

Saint Nikolai stepped forward and took Volkhova by the hand.

'Dear child, you too deserve happiness now. You will live on dry land and you will live in water. I shall make a huge river flow into Lake Ilmen, and it shall be called Volkhova. Sadko's ships will sail down this river and you will be together for ever more.' And with that Saint Nikolai led Sadko and Volkhova up, up through the water until they reached the shore.

And he was as good as his word. A mighty river flowed from the sea to Lake Ilmen and sometimes Volkhova was the river and sometimes she was the beautiful girl that Sadko had played to all those years ago. Best of all, when Sadko came up from the sea almost the first thing he did was to plant a maple tree. In time it grew a long branch, and Sadko was able to make himself a new gusle. This time, the head was a beautiful maiden with long hair and a necklace of seashells.

Russian fishermen and sailors were always careful to please the river gods and demons who might otherwise overwhelm their boats with huge waves, dragging the sailors to a watery grave. There was a real Sadko who was a rich merchant.

INDEX

BIBLIOGRAPHY

More Stories and How to Tell Them Elizabeth Clark (University of London Press, 1929)

Myths and Legends From Around the World Sandy Shepherd (Evans, 1994)

Heroes, Monsters and Other Worlds Elizabeth Warner (Peter Lowe, 1985)

Demons, Gods and Holy Men Shahrukh Husain (Peter Lowe, 1987)

Mighty Mountains Finn Bevan (Franklin Watts, 1997)

Myths and Legends of Many Lands Evelyn Smith (Thomas Nelson, 1930)

Heroes, Gods and Emperors Kerry Usher (Peter Lowe, 1983)

Warrior Gods and Spirits Douglas Gifford (Peter Lowe, 1983)

Irish Sagas and Folktales Eileen O'Faolin (Oxford University Press)

Druids, Gods and Heroes Anne Ross (Peter Lowe, 1986)

Koshka's Tales James Mayhew (Kingfisher Books, 1993)

Myths and Legends James Riordan (Hamlyn, 1987)

Sacred Skies Finn Bevan (Franklin Watts, 1997)